For Will, Nate, Sylvie, and Charlie
—H.M.Z.

Text copyright © 2006 by Harriet Ziefert
Illustrations copyright © 2006 by Amanda Haley
All rights reserved
CIP Data is available.
Published in the United States 2006 by
Blue Apple Books
515 Valley Street, Maplewood, N.J. 07040
www.blueapplebooks.com
Distributed in the U.S. by Chronicle Books

First Edition
Printed in China

ISBN 13: 978-1-59354-098-2
ISBN 10: 1-59354-098-1

3 5 7 9 10 8 6 4 2

That's What Grandmas Are For

Harriet Ziefert

pictures by Amanda Haley

 BLUE APPLE BOOKS

GRANDMA

If I forget my homework
and I call my grandma,

she will pick it up and bring it to school—
even if she has another appointment.

That's what grandmas are for.

If my mother insists on gloves and a hat,
even though only little kids wear hats and gloves,

my grandma will not
make me wear them.

That's what grandmas are for.

If I go shopping with my grandma for sports cards and I have enough money for the cards but not for the tax,

Grandma will lend me
the money I need.

If I want pizza and Grandma
would rather have Chinese food,

she will eat pizza.

That's what grandmas are for.

If I don't know the difference between
a dromedary and a Bactrian camel,
Grandma will explain. She won't say
that if I were paying attention in school,
I would know this already.

If I tell my grandma I want to
run away from home,

she will suggest a sleep-over at her house.

That's what grandmas are for.

If I want steak for breakfast and eggs for dinner, Grandma will make them for me.

If I ask for my eggs a special way, she won't complain.

She'll even ask if
I want sausage too.

Grandma loves us when we're silly
and not just when we're smart.

Grandma loves us when we're dirty and not just when we're clean.

Grandma loves us when we're difficult and not just when we're good.

That's what grandmas are for!

Grandchildren

If I feel like playing
old songs on the piano,

my grandchildren are happy
to make music with me.

That's what grandchildren are for.

If I think I've learned pretty much
everything worth knowing,

I listen to my grandchildren and learn
that there is always more to know.

If I want to read poetry out loud,
my grandson sits quietly and listens.

If I stop for gas and it's self-serve,
my granddaughter holds the nozzle.

If I am washing the car, my grandson helps rinse away the suds.

That's what grandchildren are for.

If I'm looking for a tennis
partner, my grandson turns off
the TV and plays with me.

That's what grandchildren are for.

My grandson invites me to his soccer game
and lets me take pictures from the sidelines.

After the game, he proudly introduces me to his friends.

My grandchildren make every
outing an adventure.

That's what grandchildren are for.

If I'm grumpy and my grandchildren
give me hugs, I feel better instantly.

If I don't have enough to do,
my grandchildren keep me busy.

That's what grandchildren are for.

My grandchildren love me
when I make a mistake and
not just when I'm right.

My grandchildren love me when I'm grouchy and not just when I'm nice.

If my arms are empty,
my grandchildren fill them.

That's what grandchildren are for!